Kit's Banana Split

BY MARV ALINAS • ILLUSTRATED BY KATHLEEN PETELINSEK

This is **Kit**.
Kit will make a banana **split**.

First, **Kit** must **sit**.

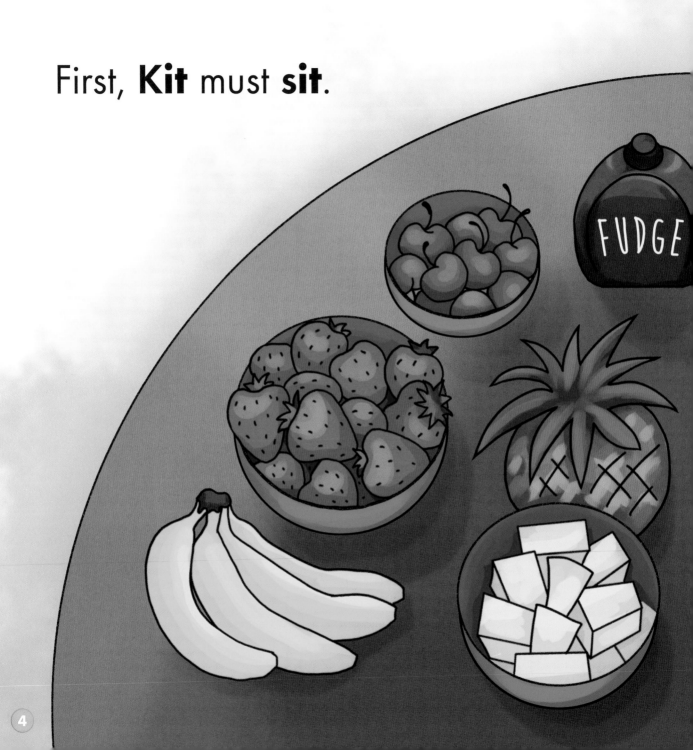

VANILLA ICE CREAM

CHOCOLATE ICE CREAM

STRAWBERRY ICE CREAM

Kit takes a banana.
It must **fit**!
Many things must **fit**
in the banana **split**.

Kit makes a **slit**.
Be careful, **Kit**!

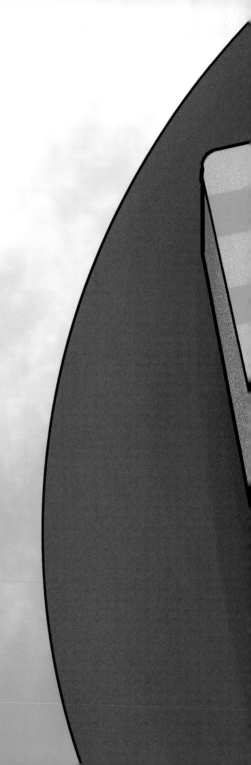

Kit takes some ice cream.
It must **fit**.
More things must **fit**
in the banana **split**!

Kit takes some fudge.
Just a little **bit**.
More things must **fit**
in the banana **split**!

Kit takes some pineapple.
Just a little **bit**.
More things must **fit**
in the banana **split**!

Kit takes some strawberries.
Just a little **bit**.
More things must **fit**
in the banana **split**!

Kit takes some whipped cream.
Just a little **bit**.
What else must **fit**
in the banana **split**?

Kit has a cherry.
She takes out the **pit**.
Now **it** is time to eat
the banana **split**!

Word List

bit   pit

fit   sit

it   slit

Kit   split

Which Words Rhyme?

About the Author

Marv Alinas has written dozens of books for children. When she's not reading or writing, Marv enjoys spending time with her husband and dogs and traveling to interesting places. Marv lives in Minnesota.

About the Illustrator

Kathleen Petelinsek has loved to draw since she was a child. Through the years, she has designed and illustrated hundreds of books for kids. She lives in Minnesota with her husband, two dogs, and new kitten.

The Child's World®
childsworld.com

Published by The Child's World®
1980 Lookout Drive • Mankato, MN 56003-1705
800-599-READ • www.childsworld.com

ISBN: 9781503823549
LCCN: 2017944773

Printed in the United States of America
PA02355